Audrey C. Welch

2008

A DAY THAT CHANGED AMERICA

GETTYSBURG

NOVEMBER 19, 1863

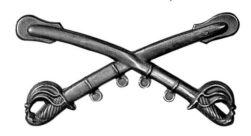

Text, Design, and Compilation
© 2003 The Madison Press Limited
Paintings © 2003 David Craig

First published in the United States by

Hyperion Books for Children
114 Fifth Avenue
New York, New York
10011-5690

First U.S. edition, 2003

1 3 5 7 9 10 8 6 4 2

Library of Congress Cataloging-in-Publication Data is on file.

ISBN 0-7868-1922-7

Printed in Singapore

A DAY THAT CHANGED AMERICA
GETTYSBURG

*The Legendary Battle and
the Address that Inspired a Nation*

TEXT BY SHELLEY TANAKA ❧ PAINTINGS BY DAVID CRAIG
Historical consultation by John Y. Simon

Hyperion Books for Children
A HYPERION / MADISON PRESS BOOK

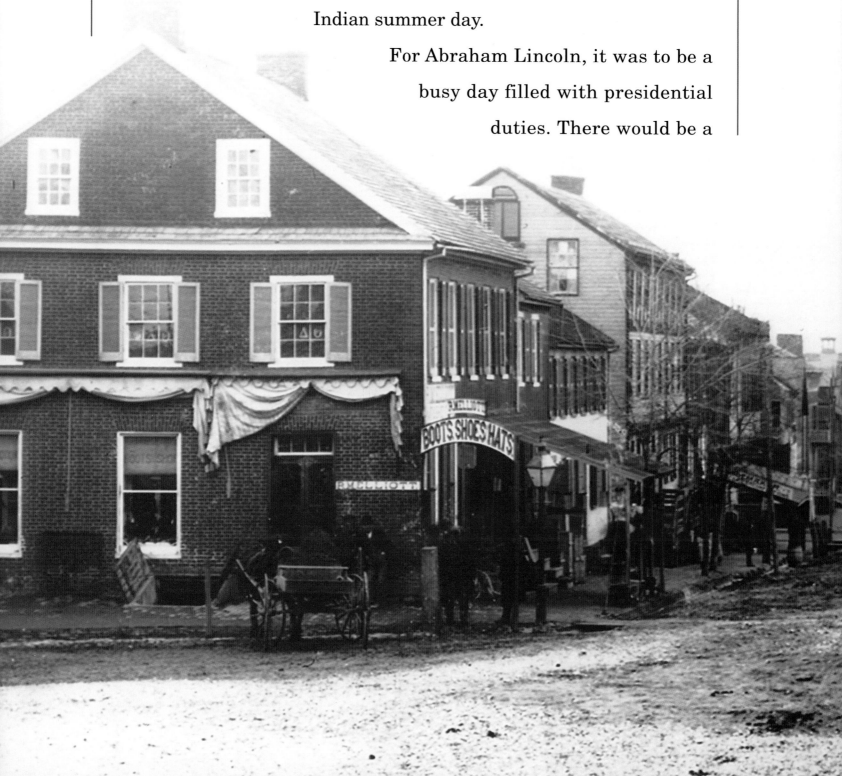

On November 19, 1863, the sky was blue over the small town of Gettysburg, Pennsylvania. It was a crisp, bright Indian summer day.

For Abraham Lincoln, it was to be a busy day filled with presidential duties. There would be a

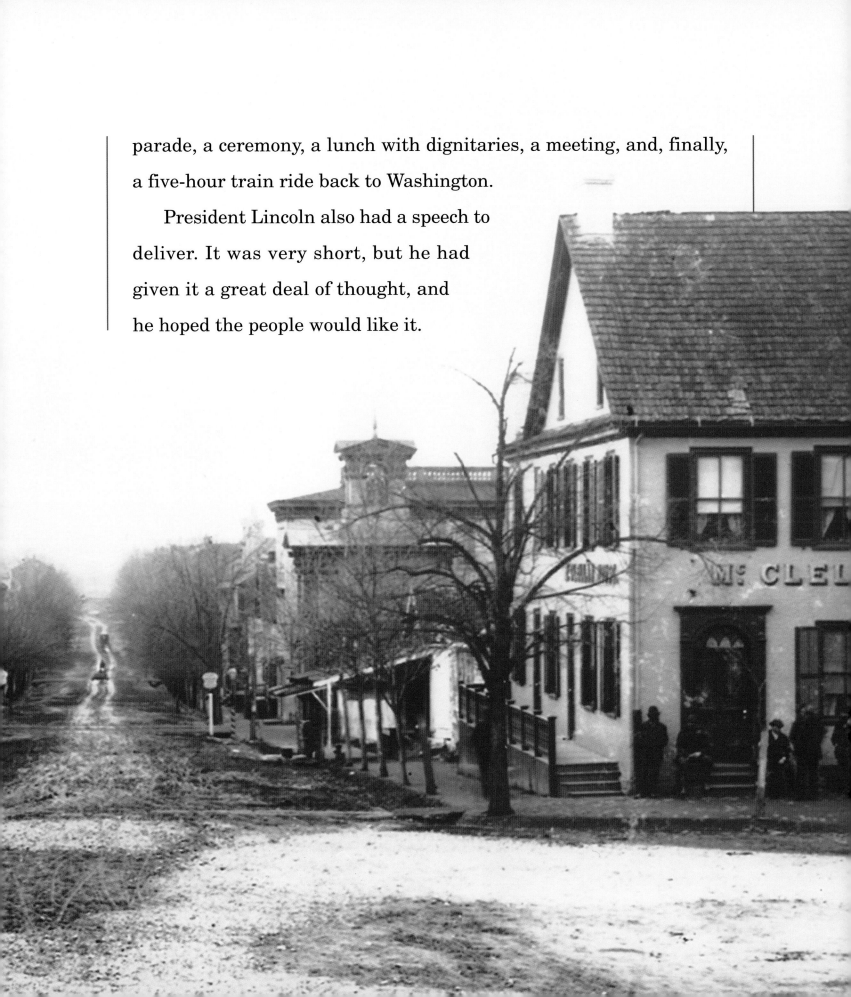

parade, a ceremony, a lunch with dignitaries, a meeting, and, finally, a five-hour train ride back to Washington.

President Lincoln also had a speech to deliver. It was very short, but he had given it a great deal of thought, and he hoped the people would like it.

CHAPTER ONE

LINCOLN *goes to* GETTYSBURG

THE PRESIDENT HAD NOT slept well. His host, David Wills, had a large, elegant home on Gettysburg's main square, but the house was full of people. Abraham Lincoln, of course, had been given a room of his own on the second floor. But the room faced the busy street and, as usual, the bed was too small, so his feet poked out over the footboard all night.

Since the President's arrival the day before, Gettysburg had been a swarm of activity. Thousands of visitors had come to see him and attend the dedication of a cemetery for soldiers who had died in the Battle of Gettysburg earlier that summer. Bands had played in the town square throughout the evening. Noisy guests had arrived at the house at all hours of the night, clattering down the halls as they crowded into every available bed.

Lincoln was tired, and he was not feeling particularly well. He had a great deal on his mind. Back in Washington, Mary Lincoln had begged her husband to cancel his trip because their ten-year-old son, Tad, had been too sick to eat his breakfast. Their older boy, Willie, had died of typhoid fever at the age of thirteen, only two years ago. They could not bear the thought of losing another son.

But Lincoln did not cancel the trip. There was a war on, and this day was too important. More than fifty thousand men had been killed, wounded, or captured at the Battle of Gettysburg.

❧

(Opposite) President Lincoln looks out the window at a crowd that has gathered outside the Wills house (right) in Gettysburg. (Above) A stovepipe hat that belonged to the President.

The Wills House, where Lincoln wrote his Gettysburg Address, Gettysburg, Pa.

Crowds in Gettysburg watch the parade to the cemetery, hoping to catch a glimpse of President Lincoln.

It was a dreadful number, even in a war where the numbers of dead and wounded had already gone beyond people's worst imaginings.

After three days of terrible fighting in early July, the Union forces had finally defeated the Confederate army. That battle had marked a turning point in a long, bloody war that had torn the country apart. Brothers were fighting against brothers, fathers against sons. Lincoln's own brother-in-law was an officer in the Confederate army.

Now Lincoln wanted to pay tribute to the soldiers who had fought for the victory at Gettysburg. He had a speech in his pocket, and he knew it was an important one. He had already rewritten it several times.

Today he would face the crowd on Cemetery Hill and remind the country why it was still at war. And he must make the people look ahead to the huge task of finishing the work the dead men had given their lives for. Together they must build a nation where one man could not own another, and all men would be free.

AT TEN O'CLOCK THE PRESIDENT JOINED AN UNTIDY PROCESSION IN THE MAIN SQUARE TO MAKE the fifteen-minute walk to the new cemetery. There were four marching bands. Several horses had been brought in to carry the dignitaries to Cemetery Hill. People pressed forward to see the President, and he shook hands with some of them. Then he mounted his

The American Civil War

The Civil War was a long, bitter, and brutal struggle between North and South. The South had an economy that depended on slave labor. As the United States expanded west, many southerners wanted to take their slaves and move to the new undeveloped territories that were preparing to become states.

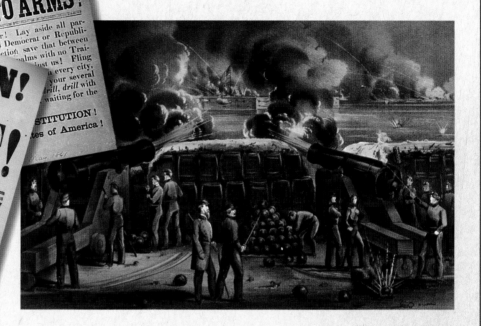

The Confederate army's attack on Fort Sumter in Charleston Harbor (above, right) marked the beginning of the Civil War. (Above) Posters in both Union and Confederate states called for volunteers to help in the fighting.

Abraham Lincoln and the Republican Party were opposed to the extension of slavery. They feared that southerners with unpaid workers would have an unfair advantage doing business in the new territories. And many hated the idea that one person could own another. When Lincoln became president, the pro-slavery states decided to leave the Union and form the Confederate States of America, so they would not be forced to change their ways.

Lincoln opposed the idea that any state could simply decide to leave the Union. He refused to surrender Fort Sumter, a Union fort in the Confederate state of South Carolina. On April 12, 1861, the Confederates attacked the fort, and the war began. By the time the Confederates surrendered four years later, 620,000 soldiers had died. The number of dead was greater than those lost by the United States in both World Wars, the Korean War, and the Vietnam War combined.

horse, looking somber and dignified in his black suit and white gloves. His tall silk hat still bore the black ribbon of mourning for his dead son.

The parade moved slowly up Baltimore Street, past the wooden houses and brick shops, many still scarred with bullet holes from the battle. The streets were thronged with people, horses, and buggies. The bands played. A regiment marched, with bayonets flashing in the sun.

By the time they were all assembled at the cemetery, more than five thousand people had gathered on the bare hilltop. There were reporters and townspeople, visitors and hospital workers. There were wounded soldiers who had fought in the battle and were still in Gettysburg recovering from their injuries.

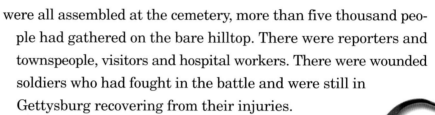

During the Battle of Gettysburg, Abraham Lincoln had been at the White House in Washington, anxiously waiting for bulletins from his generals about the progress of the fighting. He would pace up and down the room reading the dispatches. Then he would consult the map that hung on the wall, noting the spots where the battles had taken place.

Now he was in the middle of those battle sites. The fields around Gettysburg were brown and bare, the trees leafless. Yet there were still signs of where 150,000 men had met in a dreadful storm of smoke, fire, and metal. Split-rail fences lay scattered and broken. Trees were scarred black by cannon fire. The earth was still trampled, churned up by all those men and horses.

Here and there, mounds of soft earth marked the shallow graves of men who had been buried hastily where they fell. Now their bodies were being dug up and reburied in the new

⚛

(Left) This Union sergeant from New York fought at Gettysburg. He holds a rifle with a bayonet and carries a bedroll atop his knapsack. At his side is a water canteen, like the one shown above. Behind the canteen is a draft notice poster.

cemetery. Workers were trying to manage one hundred corpses a day, but it was already the middle of November. Soon the ground would freeze, making reburial impossible.

Edward Everett

Thousands had been killed or wounded on these fields. Most of them were not even professional soldiers. They were farmers, blacksmiths, teachers, factory workers, and schoolboys who had never seen battle before.

So many dead.

President Lincoln took his seat with the other guests of honor on a small wooden platform. Behind them lay the graves, spread in a semicircle.

They were all waiting for one last chair to be filled. It belonged to Edward Everett, the man who would give the main speech of the day.

But the famous orator was busy in a small tent that had been set up especially for him beside the platform. Everett had a bladder problem. He knew his speech was going to be long, and he wanted to relieve himself one last time before he stood up to give it.

Once he appeared, a chaplain recited a prayer that went on rather long. And then Everett stood up. He placed a thick sheaf of notes on a table next to him, but he did not consult them. Instead he held a big white handkerchief, which he waved grandly from time to time as he began to speak:

Standing beneath this serene sky, overlooking these broad fields...the mighty Alleghenies dimly towering before us.... We have assembled...to pay the last tribute of respect to the brave men, who, in the hard-fought battles of the first, second, and third days of July last, laid down their lives for the country on these hillsides and the plains....

— Edward Everett

Everett's strong voice carried well on the crisp fall breeze, and his words seemed to reach right across the fields to the distant hills. The crowd listened quietly while he told them the story of the Battle of Gettysburg....

CHAPTER TWO

The FORCES CONVERGE

BY JULY 1863, THE WAR HAD been going on for more than two years. There had been huge losses for both the Union and the Confederates, yet neither side had managed to turn the tide.

That summer the Confederates decided to make a bold move. General Robert E. Lee would invade the North. He would take his army up through Maryland and into Pennsylvania, drawing Union forces away from Washington. They would defeat the Union army and then move on to the capital. If they took Washington, it would be as good as winning the war.

But spies discovered Lee's plan, and the Union army immediately set out after him. Soon there were three forces moving north. On the west, the Confederate infantry was marching up the Shenandoah Valley. To the east of the Blue Ridge Mountains moved the Confederate cavalry. And behind them, in hot pursuit, came the Union army.

Soon tens of thousands of soldiers were swarming over the Pennsylvania countryside. Long columns of dusty men tramped along, their canteens clinking and their flags drooping in the stifling air. They did not advance together, because so many men would clog up the roads. Instead they marched along different roads in groups of a few thousand. When the time came to fight a battle, they would come together as an army.

General Robert E. Lee (above) was greatly respected by his Confederate soldiers. (Opposite) Lee and his troops on the way to Gettysburg.

A sketch of Union soldiers on the march, with their cannon being pulled by a team of horses. Many drawings like this one were published in newspapers at the time.

It seemed as though the land could not hold all these soldiers, their horses, wagon trains, and cannons. Some had arrived after weeks of long marches, drinking bad water and eating wormy bread, tramping through the rain in wet boots. They marched for more than thirty miles a day sometimes. Soldiers learned to walk half asleep on their feet, chewing rock-hard lumps of hardtack — a bland, gray biscuit made of flour and water. Men dropped from heatstroke, diarrhea, and bleeding feet. Even the horses and mules gave out and were abandoned on the roadside.

It was the height of summer, and Pennsylvania's farmland was rich. Blackberry bushes covered the hills, the orchards were bursting with peaches and cherries, and the forests were full of firewood. A man could walk through a field, roll heads of wheat between his hands, and chew the grains for an instant breakfast.

Yet it was hardly enough. Parties from both armies went into every town and village they passed, looking for horses, cows, chickens, coffee, whiskey, wagons, and shoes. It was only a matter of time before they reached Gettysburg, a sleepy little country town that lay like a bull's-eye at the center of ten converging roads.

It was now too evident...that the thundercloud, so long gathering blackness, would soon burst on some part of the devoted vicinity of Gettysburg.... Early in the morning on the first of July, the conflict began.

— Edward Everett

At dawn on July 1, a Union soldier on horseback spotted a division of Confederate soldiers marching along a country road west of Gettysburg. They raised their guns and fired as the rider turned his horse and fled back to town to tell the others. The battle was on.

Messages were sent to the two army commanders. General Lee was five miles west in Cashtown. The Union commander, General George Meade, was in his headquarters in Taneytown, fourteen miles to the south. They gave their orders, and soon two mighty armies were gathering and on the march. Both sides brought awesome forces — thousands upon thousands of soldiers, horses, cattle, supply wagons, and cannons — all moving toward Gettysburg.

John Burns

General George Meade

By 10:00 A.M. Union forces had gathered not far from where the first shots were fired, on a low rise of land called McPherson's Ridge. And from the west came the Confederates by the thousands, closely packed in battle formation. They outnumbered the Union defenders three to one.

The firing grew fierce as the defenders stood their ground and the Confederates inched closer, until the two sides were practically firing into each other's faces with scarcely fifty yards between them. Yet the Union troops managed to hold off the attackers, and around noon there was a break in the fighting.

The soldiers defending the ridge couldn't believe their eyes when they saw an old man trudging up the hill behind them. He was wearing a dusty blue coat with tails and shiny brass buttons, a worn black stovepipe hat, and a sand-colored vest and dark trousers. He held a musket at his side, the butt skimming the ground behind him.

The man was John Burns, a cranky sixty-nine-year-old shoemaker who lived on the west side of town. He was too old to enlist, but he had served in the War of 1812. Now there was another war right on his doorstep, and he aimed to be part of it.

That morning, he had marched out of his house and headed toward the sounds of the firing. His wife begged him not to go, but he told her to go down to the basement and stay there until he returned. His neighbors shook their heads in amazement as Burns stomped off down Chambersburg Road, but he called them chickenhearted cowards and sissies. Then he told them to look after his wife if he did not return.

He wanted to fight, but he needed a weapon. He came across a wounded soldier and asked for his musket. "What are you going to do with it?" asked the man. "Shoot some rebels," Burns replied. The soldier handed over the weapon and his box of ammunition. Burns emptied the cartridge box into his pocket and headed in the direction of McPherson's Ridge.

When he came across a regiment defending the ridge, the old man asked to see their commander. He showed the colonel his pockets bulging with ammunition and asked for permission to fight with them. The commander said yes.

When reinforcements began to arrive shortly after noon, the Confederates renewed their attack. This time they came from the north. The air was filled with the blood-chilling sound of their yells as they came yelping like hounds and splashing over the creek north of town.

General Lee arrived on the field, and he gave the signal for a full-scale attack. The Confederates charged with a fury. The Union bugles sounded the signal to retreat, but in the confusion, not everyone heard the command. One commander was shot in the throat just as he was about to give the order, and his men continued to fight hopelessly.

As the fighting became heavier, John Burns moved into a woodlot and fired from the protection of a grove of trees. By the end of the afternoon, he had been shot a number of times. Then, just as he was retreating from the shelter of the woods, he was shot in the leg. He went down, and he could not get up.

The Union soldiers did their best to hold off their pursuers as they were pushed back into town. They dragged their cannons into the main square and aimed them down the streets at the invaders. Regiments collided with each other and men scattered — climbing

✤

(Opposite) John Burns and Union soldiers attack from behind trees on McPherson's Ridge. (Above) Bugles, like this one, could be heard above the noise of battle and were used to give commands to troops over a great distance.

fences, clambering over woodpiles and slop barrels, fleeing through yards and alleys. Some tossed their rifles down wells to keep them from falling into enemy hands. Gunfire whipped through the streets, dislodging bricks and trim from houses, peppering the walls with shells.

Most of the townspeople hid in their cellars, though one woman waved her handkerchief and cheered on the defenders from her front porch. A group of young boys filled buckets and ladled out scoops of water for thirsty Union soldiers as they escaped through town.

But until reinforcements arrived, the Union forces were hugely outnumbered. Soon they had been driven right out of the south end of town.

By 5:00 P.M., both sides had had enough. Though there were several hours of daylight left, the Confederates did not press any further. The day had been hot and humid, and many soldiers had fallen from heatstroke. The streets of Gettysburg were littered with the debris of battle — muskets, swords, haversacks, canteens, hats, and the dead and wounded.

By sundown, General Lee had moved his headquarters to a stone house just west of town, and Gettysburg was in the hands of the Confederates. Some set up their cooking fires in the streets. Others pushed their way into homes looking for food and shelter. They searched cellars for hidden Union soldiers and moved the wounded into the town's churches and schools.

As the darkness deepened, the surrounding hills were lit up with soldiers' campfires. The night air was filled with the sounds of crickets and the distant strains of men singing hymns.

The streets and fields of Gettysburg were dotted with the lanterns of workers searching for the dead and wounded. Some corpses were stripped of their boots, watches, ammunition, and guns. One dead soldier was found clutching a photograph of his three young children.

But many wounded were left lying in the fields with their injuries, including John Burns. All night, the old man lay unnoticed on the edge of a woodlot behind Confederate lines, not far from General Lee's headquarters.

> *The full moon, veiled by thin clouds, shone down that night on a strangely unwonted scene. The silence of the graveyard was broken by the heavy tramp of armed men, by the neigh of the war-horse, the harsh rattle of the wheels of artillery hurrying to their stations....*
>
> — Edward Everett

The Children of the Battlefield

The soldier who was found clutching a photograph of his children was eventually identified as Private Amos Humiston of New York. After the battle, the photo was published in newspapers and magazines across the country. Copies of it were sold to raise money for the family, and a song was written in honor of the soldier and his children. Money earned by the song was used to found an orphanage in Gettysburg for children who had lost their fathers during the war. The orphanage was run by Humiston's widow, who did not find out about her husband's death until she saw the picture of her children in the newspaper in November 1863 — the same month Abraham Lincoln went to Gettysburg.

(Above) Private Amos Humiston. (Left) The photograph of his children that Humiston was holding when he died on the battlefield. (Opposite) A Union private's cap.

THAT NIGHT, UNION FORCES TOOK NEW POSITIONS ON CEMETERY HILL AND DOWN CEMETERY Ridge. Work parties moved artillery into position, chopped down trees, dug trenches, and piled rocks to create makeshift barriers.

General Meade arrived at 1:00 A.M., and reinforcements continued to stumble into the Union camps throughout the night. The incoming troops immediately fell into an exhausted sleep, huddled against the gravestones and tall pines on Cemetery Hill. Some had been marching since the previous evening. Most were too tired to raise a musket.

If the Confederates attacked at dawn, only a miracle would save them.

But dawn came, and there was no attack.

Had the contest been renewed...at daylight on the second of July...nothing but a miracle could have saved the army from great disaster. Instead of this...the day dawned, the sun rose, the cool hours of the morning passed, the forenoon and a considerable part of the afternoon wore away, without the slightest aggressive movement on the part of the enemy....

At length, between three and four o'clock in the afternoon, the work of death began.

— Edward Everett

A FIGHT *to the* DEATH

LATER, MANY SAID THE SOUTH WOULD HAVE WON THE WAR IF THEY HAD ATTACKED quickly on the morning of the second day. Instead, by the time they did make a move, the Union forces were rested and firmly positioned on the high ground.

The Union defense was lined up from Cemetery Hill along Cemetery Ridge to the hills called Little and Big Round Top. At the foot of the ridge lay an unlikely battlefield. There was a golden wheat field, a peach orchard, two tiny creeks, small meadows covered with clover and wildflowers, and some tidy woodlands. Nearby lay an eerie place the locals called Devil's Den. It was a rugged hollow littered with granite slabs and huge lichen-covered boulders, some as large as houses.

The main attack did not come until late afternoon. The day had turned thick and humid, and it was even hotter than the day before.

When the Confederates finally attacked, they surprised the Union soldiers by charging up from the south toward Devil's Den. General Lee knew that if they could make their way behind Union lines and take Little Round Top, they could turn their artillery north and mow down the enemy on Cemetery Ridge.

But it was poor terrain for fighting. Cannonballs split trees and crashed against boulders. Branches cracked under the hail of fire and crashed to the ground. A herd of cows feeding nearby was spooked by the gunfire, and the terrified beasts panicked, threatening to trample the soldiers.

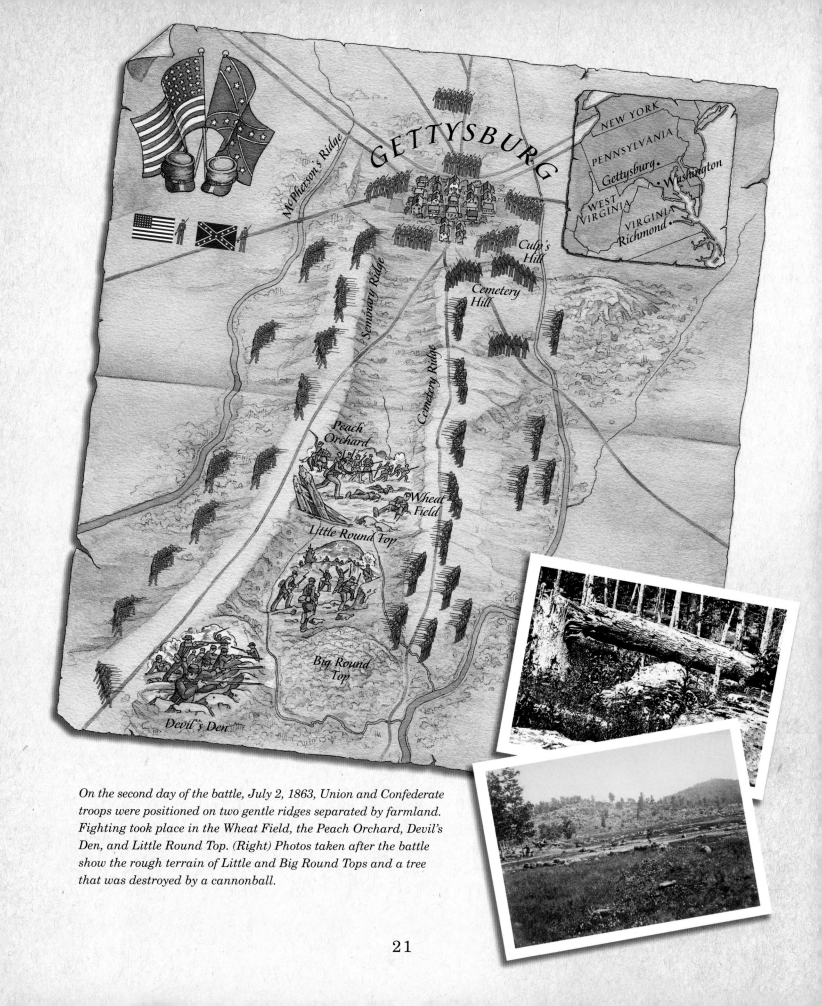

On the second day of the battle, July 2, 1863, Union and Confederate troops were positioned on two gentle ridges separated by farmland. Fighting took place in the Wheat Field, the Peach Orchard, Devil's Den, and Little Round Top. (Right) Photos taken after the battle show the rough terrain of Little and Big Round Tops and a tree that was destroyed by a cannonball.

Squeezed between ridges and orchards and woods, formations quickly split up and met the enemy in hand-to-hand fighting. Bayonets gleamed in the Wheat Field as men charged at one another. When they were too close to charge they swung their muskets by the barrels and used them as clubs. If the muskets grew too hot to handle they struck out with rammers and handspikes from the cannons, or used their fists. Shells struck rocks and exploded in a spray of flying metal. Men's faces were black from ripping open gunpowder packages with their teeth. When they ran out of ammunition, they took cartridges from the dead and wounded. Horses screamed and reared, their eyes wild, mouths foaming. The air was filled with the rotten-egg smell of sulfur from burning gunpowder.

At last, after four hours of terrible combat, the sun set and the fighting fell off. Now there was a different sound — the moans of wounded soldiers. Desperately thirsty from loss of blood, they staggered and crawled to the creeks. The water ran red with blood, but they filled their canteens and drank anyway.

The losses that day were appalling. Each side had lost almost ten thousand men. And the task of clearing the bodies was even more gruesome than it had been the night before. The full moon cast an eerie light over the trampled fields, the broken branches of the orchard, and especially the strange landscape of Devil's Den. Crippled horses had to be shot, their harnesses and saddles pulled off. Ammunition and guns had to be collected from the dead and wounded. It took half a dozen men to drag away each cannon with hooks and ropes. Bodies were lodged in crevasses, draped over boulders, half-buried in the marshy ground alongside the creeks.

Everything was stained with blood, and it was hard to tell which heaps were men or horses, and which were rocks. Most bodies had to be left where they were, and when the sky began to turn light a few hours later, farmers' hogs could be heard rooting among the dead and wounded.

But both sides were optimistic. The Union still held its position on the high ground, and General Meade was prepared to fight it out for one more day. As for General Lee, he had decided to launch a final all-out attack. "The enemy is there," he said. "And I am going to strike him."

Surely, Lee thought, it would just take one more big push to bring the Union to its knees.

(Opposite) The Confederates attack the Union troops on
July 2, 1863, in fierce hand-to-hand fighting.

GENERAL LEE HAD A PLAN. HE WOULD GATHER MOST OF THE SOUTHERN ARMY'S CANNONS TOGETHER to fire on the center of the Union line. Then, when their guns had weakened the Union defenses, he would send in the infantry — an entire division that had just arrived fresh to the battle.

The two sides lined up their cannons along both sides of the valley.

Then they waited.

From eleven till half-past one o'clock, all was still — a solemn pause of preparation, as if both armies were nerving themselves for the supreme effort. At length the awful silence, more terrible than the wildest tumult of battle, was broken by the roar of two hundred and fifty pieces of artillery from the opposite ridges....

— Edward Everett

At half past one, the two sides opened fire. The earth shook for two hours, as if the thunder of hundreds of summer storms were booming from the hills. Then it seemed to the Confederates that the Union fire was tapering off, and that they were withdrawing their cannons. But General Meade knew that a Confederate infantry attack would likely follow the lull, and he was right. His men crouched down along the length of a low stone wall at the foot of Cemetery Ridge and cocked their rifles.

When the huge clouds of billowing white cannon smoke cleared, they looked up in amazement.

Across the open field more than twelve thousand Confederate soldiers stood waiting for the order to attack. Their line stretched for a mile and a half, their muskets on their shoulders, bayonets fixed, battle flags hanging limply in the still, warm air.

The order came to advance.

"Forward! Guide center! March!"

In the bright sunlight, the line moved forward, steadily, deliberately, and in formation, precisely 110 steps per minute, across the open plain.

(Opposite) The Confederate division led by Major General George Pickett marches toward the Union lines on Cemetery Ridge. The attack later became known as Pickett's Charge.

The Union artillery let loose. The cannons on the hill had simply been maneuvering into new positions and saving their ammunition. Now they bowled down the Confederate soldiers, while the riflemen behind the stone fence picked off the open targets.

Each time a man crumpled to his knees, another moved forward to take his place. When a flag bearer went down, someone else picked up the standard and bore it defiantly. And still the marching men came on. They knew Gettysburg might be the last chance for the South to win the war, and they were determined to fight to the end.

On both sides young men stood their ground as they shot each other at close range.

Finally, only 150 yards away from the Union line, the Confederate troops simply charged desperately up the slope. But the Union fire was too much. The brigades broke apart. Some retreated. Others simply waved bits of white cloth and surrendered.

By late afternoon it was all over. Fifteen thousand Confederate soldiers had made the final charge. More than half were killed or wounded.

General Lee told his troops to prepare for a Union counterattack. But the attack never came, and by the next day the Confederates had begun to retreat. They left Gettysburg the same way they had come, west to the mountains and then south and back over the Potomac. It would be the last time they would try to invade the North.

On July 4, the rain finally came, turning the battlefields into an ugly stew of mud and death. Dead horses, men, clothing, canteens, guns, cannonballs, and broken wagons littered the ground. And the men who still lay wounded in the fields opened their mouths to the rain in relief.

Perceiving that his only safety was in rapid retreat, [General Lee] commenced withdrawing his troops at daybreak.... By nightfall, the main army was in full retreat.... An advance was accordingly made by General Meade on the morning of the 14th....

— Edward Everett

ABRAHAM LINCOLN HAD NOT BEEN IMPRESSED WITH THE EFFORTS OF GENERAL MEADE AFTER the fighting stopped. It was true that Meade had won the battle. But he did not counterattack after Pickett's Charge. He did not attack Lee before he could escape across the

Potomac, when the Confederate forces were shattered, their ammunition and food almost gone. If he had done either of these things, the war would be over by now.

But Meade had let him go. "We had them within our grasp," the President said when he heard about General Lee's retreat. "We had only to stretch forth our hands and they were ours." Instead, General Meade let the Confederates scurry away like an old woman shooing her geese across a creek. And because of that, the war was still dragging on.

(Left) Several days after the battle, Union troops leave Gettysburg in pursuit of the Confederate army. (Below) A Union officer's hat.

AS EDWARD EVERETT'S SPEECH DREW TO A CLOSE, HE RECALLED A SAYING OF THE DUKE OF Wellington, that next to a defeat, the saddest thing was a victory. No one knew this better than the citizens of Gettysburg. They had lived through the terrible days of the battle. They had seen their sons and brothers killed, their barns burned, their fields trampled, their homes plundered. Then, when the fighting stopped, they came out of their houses to help deal with the dead and wounded. They took the injured into their homes. They emptied their cupboards to feed hungry soldiers. They ripped up bedsheets and clothing for bandages.

By the end of the battle, there were twenty-one thousand wounded Union and Confederate soldiers in Gettysburg. They were packed into churches and schools. They lay on every available surface, their wounds open, their legs and arms swollen and turning black with gangrene.

Jennie Wade

It was a miracle that only one civilian citizen of Gettysburg was killed during the battle. Like many townsfolk, twenty-year-old Jennie Wade fled her home in the center of Gettysburg on the morning of July 1. With her mother and two little brothers, Jennie went to her older sister's house on Baltimore Street at the foot of Cemetery Hill. During the battle, Confederate troops fired at Union soldiers stationed on the hill. At 8:30 A.M. on July 3, Jennie was baking biscuits in the kitchen when a bullet flew through the kitchen door and killed her.

Surgeons and nurses were rushed to the town, but there were far too many wounded men to attend to. Some lay in the fields for as long as five days. When they were found, the soldiers who couldn't be saved had to be left to die while medical workers helped the men they could.

Tent hospitals were set up right in the fields, and the surgeons often operated out in the open where at least there was light. Mostly they sawed off mangled legs and arms. They gave the soldiers morphine and administered chloroform through a cattle horn held over their mouths, but there was never enough anesthetic. Limbs were piled in wagons and taken outside the town to be buried. In one part of the field, it took three hundred surgeons five days to perform the necessary amputations. Even afterward, many died anyway from infection and blood poisoning.

It took a long time to bury the dead in the rocky ground, even in temporary shallow graves. Gettysburg soon swarmed with families looking for their sons and fathers among the dead and wounded, but many bodies could not be identified.

Finally it was decided that seventeen acres of land on Cemetery Hill would be turned into a national cemetery for soldiers. At the end of October, work parties began to dig up 3,700 Union bodies and rebury them in the cemetery in plots arranged according to state. Nearly one thousand had to be buried under stones marked "Unknown." The work was not completed until the following March, and some bodies were never found at all.

Many Confederate bodies were left in the fields to rot. Some were buried in mass graves throughout the battlefield under signs that read simply "58 Rebels here." Others were later dug up and taken south to be reburied.

Bringing Home
the Dead

The huge number of dead at Gettysburg created an enormous problem. What was to be done with the thousands of bodies that lay on the battlefields? July 4 brought heavy rains, and before long the soaked bodies were covered with flies. Five thousand horses had to be burned. The smell of death was so bad that the townspeople kept their windows closed even in the heat of midsummer. Those who went out held open

Union men retrieve the bodies of their fellow soldiers for burial.

bottles of peppermint oil under their noses. People worried about disease spreading.

Work parties hurried to bury the bodies in shallow graves marked only with pieces of wood or muskets. Some were later dug up and moved to proper graves. Others were forgotten, perhaps to be eventually uncovered by rains or farmers or animals.

Many bodies were also shipped back to the soldiers' hometowns to be buried by their families. But the bodies had to be preserved if they were going to last long enough to be sent home. After the battle, embalmers found good business in Gettysburg. They would place a plank across a couple of barrels and set up shop right on the battleground.

A horse lies dead beside the Union gun carriage it was hauling.

The Battle of Gettysburg

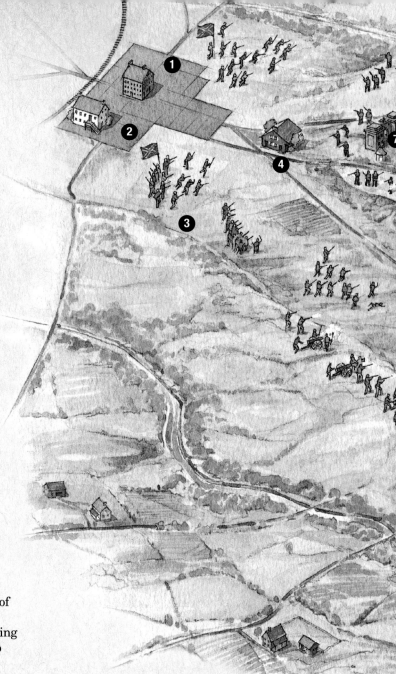

The town of Gettysburg, Pennsylvania, was founded in 1780 by James Gettys. By the 1860s it had 24,000 citizens, prosperous farms, and a thriving carriage-making industry. On the afternoon of July 1, 1863, both Confederate and Union troops marched through Gettysburg and quickly occupied areas of land surrounding the town. Several families fled from their farms as the troops moved over their properties. Many townspeople hid in their basements for fear of being caught in crossfire.

When the battle ended three days later, the town and the nearby countryside were devastated. Houses were riddled with bullets; orchards, fences, and barns were destroyed. The fields were strewn with the bodies of fallen soldiers and horses. Temporary hospitals for the more than 21,000 wounded men were set up in churches, hotels, and houses. Thousands of people arrived searching for their missing family members. The quiet town of Gettysburg was changed forever.

1. David Wills' house, where President Lincoln stayed the night before he gave the Gettysburg Address.

2. John Burns' house.

3. Seminary Ridge. Confederate soldiers fought from this high ground for the last two days of the battle. From here, they could observe the enemy lines and fire on Union troops at Cemetery Hill.

4. The house where Jennie Wade was killed by a stray bullet that came through the kitchen door.

5. Culp's Hill was occupied on the first night of the battle by Union soldiers. They dug trenches and cut down trees to use as barricades.

6. Evergreen Cemetery was built in 1858 and became known as Cemetery Hill. On the first day of battle, Union troops occupied the hill. During the fighting, they also took cover behind the gravestones.

7. The cemetery gatehouse was untouched during the battle, save for a few bullet holes.

8. Cemetery Ridge. The ridge runs more than a mile from Cemetery Hill all the way to the Round Tops. This is where Confederate troops charged at Union soldiers on July 3.

9. The Peach Orchard was held by Union troops. Their guns fired at Confederate troops to the north and south. During the fighting, the orchards were ruined, the fences were torn apart, and the barn was burned to the ground.

10. The Wheat Field. Thousands of troops fought on this field. The worst fighting took place here on the second

day of battle, which left the field and nearby woods strewn with more than 4,000 dead and wounded soldiers.

11. Little Round Top was the scene of a crucial battle on July 2. Union troops rushed to occupy the unmanned rocky hilltop and were able to fight off the advancing Confederate troops after hours of brutal fighting.

12. Big Round Top. This larger rocky hill beside Little Round Top was covered in thick woods.

13. Plum Run, the small, slow-moving stream between Little Round Top and Devil's Den.

14. Devil's Den. The huge granite boulders and steep cliffs here provided protection for the Union troops. Confederates attacked Devil's Den from all directions on the second day of battle. Many soldiers lost their way among the large rocks and mossy passages.

CHAPTER FOUR

THE PRESIDENT'S *Address*

AT LAST EDWARD EVERETT'S SPEECH came to an end. He wiped his brow with his big white handkerchief and sat down, exhausted. He had spoken for two hours. The crowd applauded loudly, and some listeners had tears in their eyes. But the audience was restless, their legs numb. Many had been standing for almost four hours, and some had wandered off

over the battlefield, skirting the horse carcasses that still lay in the field. From time to time someone would bend down to pick up a souvenir — a bullet or piece of gear, a uniform button, a belt buckle, a spent cartridge.

A choir sang a hymn. Then Abraham Lincoln stood up.

The President took his glasses out of his pocket and put them on. He took out two handwritten sheets of paper. He held them up, tilted his head to one side, and began to read. His high-pitched voice sounded shrill after Everett's deep, booming tones, but it carried well over the crowd.

"Four score and seven years ago...."

The crowd of more than five thousand people at the dedication of the new Union Cemetery at Gettysburg waits for the President to begin his speech.

"The world will little note, nor long remember, what we say here...."

The Gettysburg Address

In the Gettysburg Address, Abraham Lincoln reminded Americans that the United States was more than just a *union* of states that had joined together for political reasons. America, he said, must work together as a *nation*. The idea of the country as a nation was so important to him that he used the word five times in his speech.

Lincoln did not mention sides. He did not talk about winners and losers, or friends and enemies, or North and South. Instead, he asked people to remember why the cause of freedom was still worth fighting and dying for. And he asked them to join together in their renewed belief that free people could govern themselves and uphold the principle set out in the Declaration of Independence — that every person should have a fair and equal chance in life.

66 Four score and seven years ago our fathers brought forth upon this continent, a new nation, conceived in liberty, and dedicated to the proposition that all men are created equal.

Now we are engaged in a great civil war, testing whether that nation, or any nation so conceived and so dedicated, can long endure. We are met on a great battlefield of that war. We have come to dedicate a portion of that field, as a final resting place for those who here gave their lives, that that nation might live. It is altogether fitting and proper that we should do this.

But, in a larger sense, we cannot dedicate — we cannot consecrate — we cannot hallow — this ground. The brave men, living and dead, who struggled here, have consecrated it, far above our poor power to add or detract. The world will little note, nor long remember, what we say here, but it can never forget what they did here. It is for us, the living, rather, to be dedicated here to the unfinished work which they who fought here, have, thus far, so nobly advanced. It is rather for us to be here dedicated to the great task remaining before us — that from these honored dead we take increased devotion to that cause for which they gave the last full measure of devotion — that we here highly resolve that these dead shall not have died in vain — that this nation, under God, shall have a new birth of freedom — and that government of the people, by the people, for the people, shall not perish from the earth. 99

(Opposite) A copy of the Gettysburg Address, in Abraham Lincoln's own handwriting.

us— that from these honored dead we take increased devotion to that cause for which they here gave
the last full measure of ... 57 — that we here
highly resolve ... shall not have
... tion, under God,
... dom— and that
... eople, for the
... rath.

Four score and seven years ago our father's brought forth upon this continent, a new nation, conceived
in Liberty, and dedicated to the proposition that all
men are created equal.

Now we are engaged in a great civil war, testing
whether that nation, or any nation so conceived, and
so dedicated, can long endure, We are met on a great
battle-field of that war. We have come to dedicate
a portion of that field, as a final resting place for
those who here gave their lives, that that nation
might live. It is altogether fitting and proper that
we should do this.

But, in a larger sense, we can not dedicate—
we can not consecrate— we can not hallow—
this ground, The brave men, living and dead, who
struggled here, have consecrated it, far above our
poor power to add or detract. The world will
little note, nor long remember, what we say here, but
it can never forget what they did here, It is for us,
the living, rather, to be dedicated here to the unfinished work which they who fought here, have, thus
far, so nobly advanced. It is rather for us to be
here dedicated to the great task remaining before

THE CEREMONY WAS OVER. THE CHOIR SANG ANOTHER HYMN AND A MINISTER GAVE A CLOSING benediction. The procession walked back to town through cheering crowds, and Lincoln returned to David Wills' house for lunch. He greeted people gathered in the square and shook hands for more than an hour. He looked tired and distracted.

But there was one more thing he wanted to do before he left Gettysburg. The President had heard the story of John Burns, who had eventually returned home after lying wounded in the fields all night. Now Lincoln wanted to meet the man who had become known as the "Hero of Gettysburg."

Burns was sent for, and that afternoon the two men walked down the middle of the street to a patriotic meeting at the Presbyterian church. Abraham Lincoln listened carefully as Burns talked. John Burns no longer needed crutches to walk, but he had trouble matching Lincoln's long stride, and he looked stooped and frail next to the President.

Still, John Burns was one of the lucky ones. He was seventy years old, and he had recovered from his injuries. Many of the other wounded were not so fortunate. Even now, almost six months after the battle, they were still in Gettysburg, waiting to go home.

BY 7:00 P.M. ABRAHAM LINCOLN WAS ON HIS WAY back to Washington. It was dark as the train trundled over the Maryland countryside. There was no stopping to wave at crowds, as he had on the journey to Gettysburg the day before. No shy children reaching up with bouquets of flowers.

Instead, the President lay down on one of the side benches in the drawing-room car of the train and put a damp towel over his eyes. He did not feel well. In fact, by the

᪻

President Lincoln and John Burns
walk together to the Presbyterian church.

time the train pulled into Washington at midnight, he had a fever. A mild form of small-pox, his doctor said, and for the next three weeks, he rested quietly in the White House.

But the country was alerted to his Gettysburg Address as the text of his speech hit the telegraph wires, and newspapers across the country printed their comments. Though his political opponents immediately attacked the speech ("Silly, flat, and dishwatery," one said), the verdicts became more thoughtful as Lincoln's words were examined more closely. "Turn back and read it over," advised one journalist. "It will repay study as a model speech. Strong feelings and a large brain were its parents."

One admirer of the speech was Edward Everett, who wrote to the President, "I should be glad, if I could flatter myself that I came as near to the central idea of the occasion in two hours, as you did in two minutes."

Meanwhile, back in Gettysburg, workers moved over the fields with their shovels and wagons, as the grim work of collecting and reburying the dead continued.

A Speech that Inspired a Nation

Edward Everett and Abraham Lincoln could not have given more different speeches at Gettysburg. Everett spent a great deal of time writing his speech. In fact, the ceremony was delayed by four weeks because he needed more time to prepare it. His speech was two hours long, sometimes flowery, and full of names, facts, and historical references. His deep voice thundered over the crowd, and he waved his arms grandly as he recited the whole text from memory. It was an impressive performance.

Abraham Lincoln's speech was two minutes long. It was handwritten on two sheets of paper that he held in front of him while he read. Most of the words had only one syllable. He did not have much time to prepare his speech, as he had only been asked to speak at the Gettysburg memorial a few weeks before the ceremony, but the ideas had been in his mind for quite some time.

Edward Everett was a former president of Harvard — a man with a vast formal education. Abraham Lincoln had gone to school for less than one year. Yet both men were avid readers, and they both loved language. They borrowed phrases and drew on a wide knowledge of literature and history that went back to the ancient Greeks, the Bible, and Shakespeare.

Few speakers since have been able to match their eloquence. Some have called Lincoln the last president who could truly use words. In fact, no American president has written his own speeches for fifty years. On September 11, 2002, the anniversary of the terrorist attacks in New York City and Washington D.C. the year before, a number of politicians chose to recite Lincoln's Gettysburg Address as a model of a simple, powerful speech that calls on Americans to stand together in difficult times.

Gettysburg Legends

When we look back on great events in history, we want to know everything we can about that moment. So it was with Lincoln's Gettysburg Address. As soon as people realized what a remarkable speech he had made, the rush was on to reconstruct every detail surrounding it. When did he compose it? Exactly how many words did he use? How did he feel after he gave it?

Legends grew. The most famous story, now known to be untrue, was that Lincoln composed the speech on the train to Gettysburg on November 18, scribbling it down on an envelope balanced on his knee while the train rocked over the rails. Some claimed that he was placed on a too-small horse riding to the ceremony, and looked "ungainly." Others said that he was disappointed with the speech. Still others reported that he finished speaking before a photographer could even take his picture.

Whole books have been written about these two minutes in history. The fact is that no one knows for sure the complete truth about many of these moments. There are no films or recordings. But, as many historians have pointed out, does it matter? On that day, Abraham Lincoln delivered a speech that, over time, has become the most memorable in American history.

Many illustrators have created fanciful depictions of Lincoln giving his famous speech.

(Opposite) This photograph, taken in 1864, was used for the image of Lincoln that is now engraved on the U.S. one-cent coin. (Above) The only known photograph of President Lincoln during the dedication ceremony at Gettysburg was taken just after he sat down following his speech.

Remembering GETTYSBURG

T HE BATTLE OF GETTYSBURG WAS THE BIGGEST AND BLOODIEST BATTLE OF THE ENTIRE Civil War. But the war continued — and during the next twenty months 300,000 more lives were lost. By the end of the war, 620,000 soldiers had died. The same number had been wounded, and the civilian casualties were uncounted.

On April 9, 1865, Robert E. Lee finally surrendered, and the war was over. Five days later, Abraham Lincoln was fatally shot in the back of the head by a crazed actor as part of a plot to avenge the South. The end of the war marked the beginning of new struggles. Huge areas of the South were on the verge of starvation. Slavery was outlawed, but the former slaves now had no land, education, homes, or jobs. And as black people tried to make new lives for themselves, they met with new prejudices in both the North and the South.

AFTER THE WAR, JOHN BURNS TOLD HIS STORY MANY TIMES, AND HE RECEIVED A GREAT DEAL OF attention from the press. Many claimed to have seen him in battle that afternoon, and exciting stories abounded. That he had nearly been hung for being a combatant out of uniform. That after he was injured, he had used his penknife to bury his weapon so that it wouldn't fall into enemy hands. That he had limped off the battlefield using his musket as a crutch.

It is almost impossible to prove the truth of these stories. And not everyone was a fan of John Burns. Many people in Gettysburg resented the attention that was showered upon him at the expense of their own contributions to the battle.

John Burns was granted a special military pension before his death in 1872. In 1903, a monument was dedicated to his memory. It was placed not far from the spot where he first offered his services to the Union forces on McPherson's Ridge. A plaque on the front of Gettysburg Presbyterian Church commemorates his meeting with Abraham Lincoln on November 19, 1863.

A lone cannon stands guard at Gettysburg National Military Park. Today, the battlefield is preserved as a memorial to the soldiers who fought and died there.

TODAY THE FIELDS AROUND GETTYSBURG FORM Gettysburg National Military Park. It is a huge outdoor museum spread over rolling hills, woodlands, fields, and orchards. Cannons line the top of Seminary Ridge. In some places you can still see the trench lines of the battle. And from time to time, farm plows still uncover the

odd bullet, shell — or bone. Hundreds of statues, monuments, and plaques dot the countryside, marking the spots where a regiment made a stand, or a general was killed. It is the best-marked battlefield in the world.

In 1913, on the fiftieth anniversary of the battle, 57,000 veterans from both sides returned to Gettysburg. By now they were old men. They stayed in a huge tent city and shared meals together. They lined up and shook hands over the stone wall that had separated the two sides during the Confederates' last desperate charge. And they remembered their fallen comrades.

❧

(Above) A statue of Union General Gouverneur Kemble Warren, who held Little Round Top, looks out over the battlefield. (Right) In the summer of 1913, fifty years after the Battle of Gettysburg, a group of Confederate survivors reenacted Pickett's Charge. (Insets) Union and Confederate veterans meet and reminisce at the reunion.

GLOSSARY

amputation: the act of cutting a limb from the body.

anesthetic: a substance that causes unconsciousness or numbness, and is used by surgeons in performing operations.

artillery: weapons such as large guns and cannons.

bayonet: a sharp steel blade attached to the end of a rifle.

cartridge: a paper tube containing gunpowder and a lead ball.

cavalry: a group of soldiers on horseback. A cavalry **regiment** was composed of 300–400 men.

chloroform: a liquid **anesthetic** once used on patients undergoing surgery.

embalmer: a person who treats a dead body to keep it from decaying.

gangrene: a condition in which loss of blood causes skin and flesh to rot.

handspike: a bar used as a lever for moving a cannon.

infantry: foot soldiers who are trained and ready for battle.

morphine: a mild **anesthetic**.

musket: a large gun that is carried on a soldier's shoulder and loaded with a **cartridge** through

the muzzle at the end of the gun barrel.

rammer: a rod for pushing the charge into a cannon. Also called a ramrod.

regiment: a unit of about 400–1000 soldiers. A brigade is composed of four or more regiments; a division, of two or three brigades; a corps, of two or more divisions; and an army, of a multitude of corps.

reinforcements: soldiers sent to strengthen an army.

telegraph: a machine used to communicate messages over long distances using coded signals.

INDEX

Page numbers in italics refer to illustrations or maps.

A
Amputations, 28
Anesthetic
    lack of, 28

B
Battle of Gettysburg, 7, 10, *30–31*, 42
    begins, 15
    casualties, 7–8, 23, 28
    civilian casualty, 28, *28*
    Confederate defeat at, 8, 26
    Confederate forces attack, 15, 20, 24–26, *25*
    Confederate retreat from, 26, 27
    Confederate strategy, 12

Confederate troop positions, *21*, 24, *30, 31*
coping with the dead, 18, 23, 28, 29
effects on landscape, 10, 20, *21*, 26
50th anniversary, 44
fighting during, 16–18, *22*, 23, 24–26
pre-battle conditions, 14
search for dead and wounded, 18, 23, 27–28, 29
troop movements, 12
Union defense positions, 20, 21, 23, 24, 26, *30, 31*
Union forces during, 8, *14*, 15, 18–19, 20
Union soldiers fight in, 15–16, *17*
veterans of, 44, *44–45*
wounded in, 10, 18, 27–28, 38

Big Round Top, 20, *21*, 31
Blue Ridge Mountains, 12
Bugles, in battle, 16, *16*
Burns, John, 15, *15*, 18.
    See also "Hero of Gettysburg."
    dies, 42
    house of, *30*
    is wounded, 16
    joins battle, 16, *17*
    legends surrounding, 42
    meeting with Lincoln commemorated, 42
    meets Lincoln, 38, *38*
    monument to, 42

C
Cannon, *14*, 15, 24, 26, *43*
Cashtown, 15
Casualties, 7–8, 9, 23, 28, 42
Cemetery Hill, 8, 19, 20, 28, *30*

Cemetery Ridge, 19, 20, 24, *25, 31*
Charleston Harbor, *9*
Civil War
    begins, 9
    biggest battle of, 42
    casualties, 9, 42
    ends, 42
    reasons for, 9
    South's last chance to win, 26
    stalemate during, 12
Confederate
    army attacks Fort Sumter, 9, *9*
    dead, 28, 29
    States of America, 9
    veterans, 44, *44–45*
Confederates, 9, 12, 15, 16, 18, 19, 20, *21, 22*, 27, 30. *See also* Confederate.
Culp's Hill, *30*

D
Dead. *See also* Casualties.
  graves of, 10, 11, 28, 29, *29*
  reburial of, 10–11, 28,
    29, 39
Declaration of
  Independence, 36
Devil's Den, 20, *21*, 23, *31*
Duke of Wellington, 27

E
Embalmers, 29
Everett, Edward, 11, *11*,
  27, 39
  begins speech, 11
  ends speech, 32
  excerpts from speech,
    11, 14, 18, 20, 24, 26
  praises Lincoln's
    speech, 39
  speech compared to
    Lincoln's, 39
Evergreen Cemetery, *30*

F
Fort Sumter
  attack on, 9, *9*

G
Gettys, James, 30
Gettysburg, 4, 7,
    10 15, 18, 19, *20*, 26,
    27, 28, *29*, 30, 41, 42, 44
  Baltimore Street, 10, 28
  Chambersburg Road, 16
  in Confederate hands, 18
  position of, 14, *21*
  townspeople of, 18,
    27–28, 29
  troops march to, 14
Gettysburg Address.
    See also Lincoln,
    Abraham, speech.
  ideas presented in, 36
  Lincoln's preparation
    for, 39
  Lincoln reads, 33, *34–35*
  response to, 39, 41
  text of, 36, *37*

Gettysburg cemetery
  dedication of, 7–8,
    10–11, 33, *32–33*
Gettysburg National
    Military Park, *43*, 44
Gettysburg orphanage, 19
Gettysburg Presbyterian
    Church, 38, 42

H
"Hero of Gettysburg," 38.
    See also Burns, John.
Horses
  dead, 26, 29, *29*, 30, 33
  injured, 23
  Lincoln's, 8, 41
Hospitals, 28, 30
Humiston, Private Amos,
    19, *19*
  children of, 19, *19*
  widow of, 19

K
Korean War, 9

L
Lee, General Robert E.,
    12, *12*, *13*, 15, 18, 20, 26
  headquarters of, 18
  invades the North, 12
  plans final attack, 24
  retreats from
    Gettysburg, 27
  signals attack, 16
  surrenders, 42
Lincoln, Abraham, 8, 10,
    11, 19, 27, 36, *40*
  at David Wills' house,
    6, 7, *30*, 38
  disappointment with
    Meade, 27
  during Battle of
    Gettysburg, 10
  eloquence of, 39
  illness of, 38–39
  killed, 42
  meets John Burns, 38, *38*
  opposes slavery, 9

presidential duties, 4–5
returns to Washington, 38
speech, 5, 8, 33, 36, *37*,
  39. *See also*
  Gettysburg Address.
speech compared to
  Everett's, 39
speech, legends
  surrounding, 41, *41*
visit to Gettysburg, 4–5,
  7–8, 10–11, 19, 38
Lincoln, Mary, 7
Lincoln, Tad, 7
Lincoln, Willie, 7
Little Round Top, 20, *21*,
  31, *44*

M
Maryland, 12, 38
McPherson's Ridge, 15,
  16, 24
Meade, General George,
  15, *15*, 19, 23, 24
  fails to counterattack,
    26, 27

N
New York, *10*, 19
New York City
  terrorist attack on, 39
North, 9, 15, 36, 42
  invaded by South, 12, 26
Nurses, 28

P
Parade
  to cemetery, 8, *8*, 10
Peach Orchard, 20, *21*,
  22, *31*
Pennsylvania, 4, 12, 14
Pickett, Major
  General George
  arrives with fresh
    troops, 24, *25*
  last charge, 27, 44,
    44–45

Plum Run, *31*
Potomac, 26, 27
President Lincoln. *See*
    Lincoln, Abraham.

R
Republican Party, 9

S
Seminary Ridge, *30*, 44
Shakespeare, 39
Shenandoah Valley, 12
Slavery, 9, 42
Soldier's equipment, *10*
South, 9, 15, 20, 26, 28,
  36, 42
  plot to avenge, 42
South Carolina, 9
Surgeons, 28

T
Taneytown, 15

U
Union, 9, 12, 23, *21*, *22*, 30
  army, 12
  dead, burial of, 28, 29, *29*
  spies, 12
United States. *See* Union.

V
Veterans, 44, *44–45*
Vietnam War, 9

W
Wade, Jennie, 28, 28
  house of, *30*
War of 1812, 15
Warren, General
    Gouverneur Kemble, *44*
Washington D.C., 5, 7, 10,
  12, 38
  terrorist attack on, 39
Wheat Field, *21*, *22*, 23, *31*
White House, 10, 39
Wills, David, 7
  house of, 7, *7*, *30*, 38
World Wars, 9

PICTURE CREDITS

All paintings are by David Craig unless otherwise indicated. All maps are by Jack McMaster.

C/M — CORBIS/MAGMA
DT — Don Troiani, www.historicalprints.com
LC — Library of Congress
NARA — National Archives and Records Administration
PH — Picture History

Front flap: DT.
1: DT.
4–5: Adams County Historical Society, Gettysburg, Pennsylvania.
7: (Left) Bettmann/C/M. (Right) PH.
8: NARA.
9: (Inset, top) Museum of Connecticut History. (Inset, bottom and right) C/M.
10: (Left) C/M. (Right) Tria Giovan/C/M.
11: LC.
12: LC.
14: LC.
15: (Left) PH. (Right) Medford Historical Society Collection/C/M.
16: DT.
18: DT.
19: Mark H. Dunkelman Collection.
21: (Top inset) LC. (Bottom inset) C/M.
27: (Left) C/M. (Right) DT.
28: National Park Service, Gettysburg National Military Park.
29: (Top) Bettmann/C/M. (Bottom) C/M.
32–33: NARA.
37: Courtesy of the Illinois State Historical Library.
40: C/M.
41: (Top and inset) Bettmann/C/M. (Bottom) C/M.
43: W. Cody/C/M.
44: (Left) David Muench/C/M.
44–45: Pennsylvania State Archives, RG-25 Records of Special Commissions, Fiftieth Anniversary of the Battle of Gettysburg, Pickett's Charge of July 3, 1913.
45: (Inset, left) LC. (Inset, right) Brown Brothers.

RECOMMENDED READING

For young readers:

Abraham Lincoln's Gettysburg Address: Four Score and More by Barbara Silberdick Feinberg (Twenty First Century Books). An in-depth discussion of the famous speech.

The Battle of Gettysburg in American History by Ann Graham Gaines (Enslow Publishers). Highlights personal stories and examines the causes of the battle and the events surrounding it.

My Brother's Keeper: Virginia's Diary, Gettysburg, Pennsylvania, 1863 by Mary Pope Osborne and Will Osborne (Scholastic). A gripping account of the battle through the eyes of a young girl.

For older readers:

American Heritage History of the Battle of Gettysburg by Craig L. Symonds (HarperCollins). A thorough chronicle and analysis of the three-day battle, from beginning to end.

WEBSITES

Gettysburg National Military Park www.nps.gov/gett

CivilWar.com www.civilwar.com

ACKNOWLEDGMENTS

The author and Madison Press Books would like to thank Craig L. Symonds, the author of several books on the Civil War, and Peter Monahan at the Civil War Headquarters in Gettysburg for their kind assistance. The story of John Burns is based on information found in *John Burns: "The Hero of Gettysburg"* by Timothy H. Smith.

Editorial Director:
Hugh M. Brewster

Associate Editorial Director:
Wanda Nowakowska

Project Editor:
Kate Calder

Editorial Assistance:
Imoinda Romain

Graphic Designer:
Jennifer Lum

Production Director:
Susan Barrable

Production Manager:
Donna Chong

Color Separation:
Colour Technologies

Printing and Binding:
Tien Wah Press

GETTYSBURG was produced by Madison Press Books, which is under the direction of Albert E. Cummings.

Madison Press Books
1000 Yonge Street, Suite 200, Toronto, Ontario, Canada, M4W 2K2